THE SURVIVOR TREE

by

Gaye Sanders

illustrations by Pamela Behrend

THE ROADRUNNER PRESS
OKLAHOMA CITY, OKLAHOMA

Published by The RoadRunner Press

A portion of the proceeds from this book will go to the
Oklahoma City National Memorial and Museum.

Catalog-in-Publication Data is on file at OCLC and SkyRiver and viewable at www.WorldCat.org
Library of Congress Control Number: 2017953498

ISBN: 978-1-937054-49-6

First Edition printed December 2017 in the United States of America

10 9 8 7 6 5 4 3 2 1

for the ones we lost on April 19, 1995

Nearly one hundred years ago, I was a tiny cutting from a great American elm. A loving family planted me in their yard as the horses and wagons clip-clopped along the dirt roads of a young town on the Oklahoma prairie called Oklahoma City.

That day was the beginning of my story.

The children and I grew up together as this new American city grew bigger and bigger all around us. Gravel roads became paved streets. Streetcars and automobiles replaced horses and buggies. Men built buildings so tall they were called skyscrapers because they seemed to touch the Oklahoma sky.

Those were exciting days.

As the years went by, I learned some days bring sadness. The family that loved and cared for me outgrew their home and had to move away.

When moving day came, I gave them my comfort and shade one last time as one by one, they hugged me and waved good-bye.

That day left me all alone for the first time.

Before long, enormous machines rumbled in and gobbled up the old house like goats eating a tasty snack. Then workers with hammers and nails came to build something new.

Every day, the workers would seek out my shade as they ate lunch or napped on break.

Those were productive days.

One afternoon when the building was nearly finished, I overheard the workers talking about me as they ate their sandwiches nearby.

The boss says this tree's got to go.

We can't cut this tree down. It's the only shade around!

Their words worried me, but no one cut me down that day.

I was still standing on March 22, 1977, when the building opened with a big celebration. The new building was given a name that day—the Alfred P. Murrah Federal Building.

The Murrah Building was such a busy place. Every day, all day long, people scurried in and out—men and women in suits who helped keep our country running, ordinary Americans and visitors who needed Uncle Sam's help, and the men and women in uniform who served in order to keep our country safe.

Best of all were the many children from the little day care inside the Murrah Building who came each day to laugh and sing and play under my branches. I always stretched my boughs extra wide for them so everybody had a shady spot out of the hot Oklahoma sun, including the nice lady with the big red hat who liked to come and eat her lunch with me.

Those were useful days.

One bright April morning as I waited for the children to come out and play, I watched as the city started another day.

I did not feel the hate in the air.

And I did not notice the big yellow truck parked so near the building.

Boom!

The ground beneath my roots shook, and windows across the city shattered. The explosion was so loud, people heard it more than fifty miles away.

Then . . . silence.

That was the day the clocks stopped at 9:02 a.m.

What I saw next was stranger still. People did not run away from the burning Murrah Building. People ran toward it.

And then I realized. They were running to help the people inside.

That was a day for courage.

Help came first from Oklahoma but then from everywhere. By the end of that day, first responders from Arizona and New York had arrived. The first responders brought

rescue dogs, wearing little shoes on their paws to avoid injury. Dogs and handlers searched tirelessly through the mountain of rubble as day turned to night and back again.

One by one, the weary rescue workers and their canine helpers came and rested against my trunk, only to go back to search some more.

My charred branches had no shade to offer them.

Still, I was glad to give them what comfort I could that day.

Like so many in Oklahoma City, I was not sure I would survive the bombing. That is what it had been, the loud noise that shook our city that April morning, a homemade bomb hidden in a yellow moving truck, left there by a young man who let hate fill his heart.

The young man would be caught and would pay for his crime. Our city would be left to deal with the destruction the young man had left behind.

Once again, the calls came to cut me down.

It's gotta come down. There's evidence in those branches, one man said.

Look at it, another worker said. *It's barely standing. It'll come down soon enough on its own.*

A third, with amazement in his eyes, whispered, *I can't believe it is still here.*

They did not cut me down that day. Instead, in short order, they climbed into my blackened branches and gently removed the debris and evidence that had collected there.

Did they know I was alive that day?

What was left of the Murrah Building was put under a big, bright spotlight. And a fence went up to keep the area safe. And then, to everyone's surprise, the people began to come to the fence—twenty-four hours a day, rain or shine.

I watched as the visitors comforted one another and tied messages and keepsakes to the fence. Teddy bears. Photographs. American flags. A single red rose. A fireman's hat. A child's drawing. Letters both long and short.

The gifts filled the fence not once but over and over and over again. Each and every one was carefully saved when its time on the fence was over.

Then 33 days, 21 hours, and 59 minutes after the day the city went silent, America gathered to watch the last remnants of the Murrah Building come thundering to the ground. No one would ever again have to look at the gaping wound that hate had wrought.

But the fence. It stayed. And the people—they still came.

Those were healing days.

The first summer after the bombing was followed by the first fall. The trees in the neighborhood turned bright with color and then were softly covered in the snows of the first winter.

Through it all, I stood charred and alone.

Waiting.

Those were uncertain days.

I felt the warmth of spring arrive and the buds well up in my branches. I knew before anyone could tell me that I was healing just as the people of Oklahoma City were healing.

When my first leaf appeared, it caused quite a stir.

The tree! It survived!

That was a day of promise.

The news spread like an Oklahoma wildfire through the city . . . the country . . . and then the whole world. People began to call me "the Survivor Tree."

The people still came to the fence, but now they also came to see me, as once the little children and the nice lady had done. They said I gave them hope that they, too, could survive, despite what had happened.

My days had purpose once again.

When we gathered that first April to remember the 168 people we lost on the nineteenth day of April 1995, I was there, as I had always been.

I was a tree that love had planted.

I had become a symbol that love will always conquer hate.

The families left that day with seedlings from me to plant at home, a remembrance of their loved ones and a tradition still followed to this day.

My offspring now grow in every state in the union including on hallowed ground at the memorial site of the September 11, 2001, attacks on the World Trade Center in New York City.

It has been many years since the world went silent that beautiful clear April morn, but every single day, the people still come.

Below me, a tranquil memorial park now stands, with 168 chairs—one for each person we lost that day. One is for the nice lady who no longer comes for lunch. Nineteen smaller chairs, for the children who once played beneath my shade. And one, for the nurse who chose to run toward danger on that fateful day.

People from all over the world come now to stand by me and remember. They mourn what was done in the name of hate and what we lost that day. And as they wipe away their tears, they vow to never let such an act of hatred happen again.

They leave promising to teach their children the power of love and tolerance. I watch them go and know our world will be better for them having come here to see this place, to learn about what happened on April 19, 1995.

A day we promise never to forget.

In Memoriam

Lucio Aleman, Jr.	Peola Battle	Peachlyn Bradley
Teresa Antionette Alexander	Danielle Nicole Bell	Woodrow Clifford "Woody" Brady
Richard A. Allen	Oleta C. Biddy	Cynthia L. Brown
Ted L. Allen	Shelly D. Bland	Paul Gregory Beatty Broxterman
Miss Baylee Almon	Andrea Yvette Blanton	Gabreon D. L. Bruce
Diane E. (Hollingsworth) Althouse	Olen Burl Bloomer	Kimberly Ruth Burgess
Rebecca Needham Anderson	Sgt. First Class Lola Bolden, U.S. Army	David Neil Burkett
Pamela Cleveland Argo	James E. Boles	Donald Earl Burns, Sr.
Saundra G. (Sandy) Avery	Mark Allen Bolte	Karen Gist Carr
Peter R. Avillanoza	Casandra Kay Booker	Michael Carrillo
Calvin Battle	Carol Louise Bowers	Zackary Taylor Chavez

The spirit of this city and this nation will not be defeated; our deeply rooted faith sustains us. — **inscription on Survivor Tree wall**

Robert N. Chipman	Katherine Louise Cregan	Carrol June "Chip" Fields
Kimberly Kay Clark	Richard (Dick) Cummins	Kathy A. Finley
Dr. Margaret L. "Peggy" Clark	Steven Douglas Curry	Judy J. (Froh) Fisher
Anthony Christopher Cooper II	Brenda Faye Daniels	Linda Louise Florence
Antonio Ansara Cooper, Jr.	Sgt. Benjamin LaRanzo Davis, USMC	Don Fritzler
Dana LeAnne Cooper	Diana Lynne Day	Mary Anne Fritzler
Harley Richard Cottingham	Peter L. DeMaster	Tevin D'Aundrae Garrett
Kim R. Cousins	Castine Brooks Hearn Deveroux	Laura Jane Garrison
Aaron M. Coverdale	Tylor Santoi Eaves	Jamie (Fialkowski) Genzer
Elijah S. Coverdale	Ashley Megan Eckles	Sheila R. Gigger-Driver
Jaci Rae Coyne	Susan Jane Ferrell	Margaret Betterton Goodson

In Memoriam

Kevin "Lee" Gottshall II
Ethel L. Griffin
J. Colleen Guiles
Capt. Randolph A. Guzman, USMC
Cheryl E. Hammon
Ronald Vernon Harding, Sr.
Thomas Lynn Hawthorne, Sr.
Doris "Adele" Higginbottom
Anita Christine Hightower
Thompson Eugene "Gene" Hodges, Jr.
Peggy Louise Holland
Linda Coleen Housley
Dr. George Michael Howard, DVM
Wanda Lee Howell
Robbin Ann Huff
Dr. Charles E. Hurlburt
Jean Nutting Hurlburt
Paul D. Ice
Christi Yolanda Jenkins
Norma "Jean" Johnson
Raymond "Lee" Johnson
Larry James Jones
Alvin J. Justes
Blake Ryan Kennedy
Carole Sue Khalil
Valerie Jo Koelsch
Ann Kreymborg
Rona Linn Kuehner-Chafey
Teresa Lea Taylor Lauderdale
Mary Leasure-Rentie
Kathy Cagle Leinen
Carrie Ann Lenz
Donald Ray Leonard
LaKesha Richardson Levy

Dominique Ravae (Johnson) – London
Rheta Bender Long
Michael L. Loudenslager
Aurelia Donna Luster
Robert Lee Luster, Jr.
Mickey B. Maroney
James K. Martin
Rev. Gilbert X. Martinez
James A. McCarthy II
Kenneth Glenn McCullough
Betsy J. (Beebe) McGonnell
Linda G. McKinney
Cartney J. McRaven
Claude Arthur Medearis, SSA
Claudette (Duke) Meek
Frankie Ann Merrell
Derwin W. Miller
Eula Leigh Mitchell
John C. Moss III
Ronota Ann Newberry-Woodbridge
Patricia Ann Nix
Jerry Lee Parker
Jill Diane Randolph
Michelle A. Reeder
Terry Smith Rees
Antonio "Tony" C. Reyes
Kathryn Elizabeth Ridley
Trudy Jean Rigney
Claudine Ritter
Christy Rosas
Sonja Lynn Sanders
Lanny Lee David Scroggins
Kathy Lynn Seidl
Leora Lee Sells

Karan Howell Shepherd
Chase Dalton Smith
Colton Wade Smith
Victoria (Vickey) L. Sohn
John Thomas Stewart
Dolores (Dee) Stratton
Emilio Tapia
Victoria Jeanette Texter
Charlotte Andrea Lewis Thomas
Michael George Thompson
Virginia M. Thompson
Kayla Marie Titsworth
Rick L. Tomlin
LaRue A. Treanor
Luther H. Treanor
Larry L. Turner
Jules A. Valdez
John Karl Van Ess III
Johnny Allen Wade
David Jack Walker
Robert N. Walker, Jr.
Wanda Lee Watkins
Michael D. Weaver
Julie Marie Welch
Robert G. Westberry
Alan G. Whicher
Jo Ann Whittenberg
Frances "Fran" Ann Williams
Scott D. Williams
W. Stephen Williams
Clarence Eugene Wilson, Sr.
Sharon Louise Wood-Chesnut
Tresia Jo "Mathes" Worton
John A. Youngblood

The bombing killed 168 people and injured more than 800. Rebecca Anderson, a nurse, died while helping the wounded. She is included in the 168. Three of the women who died were pregnant: Sheila R. Gigger-Driver, Carrie Ann Lenz, and Robbin Ann Huff. Gigger-Driver planned to call her baby Gregory N. Driver II; Lenz planned to call her baby Michael James Lenz III; and Robbin Huff planned to call her baby Amber Denise Huff.

The Oklahoma City Bombing
April 19, 1995
9:02 a.m.

we will never forget